Nina
the Birthday Cake Fairy

For Magical Myla Ramsden

Lancashire Library Services

30118126416985

PETERS	JF
£4.99	19-Apr-2013

ORCHARD BOOKS
338 Euston Road, London NW1 3BH
Orchard Books Australia
Level 17/207 Kent Street, Sydney, NSW 2000
A Paperback Original

First published in 2013 by Orchard Books

© 2013 Rainbow Magic Limited.
A HIT Entertainment company. Rainbow Magic
is a trademark of Rainbow Magic Limited.
Reg. U.S. Pat. & Tm. Off. And other countries.

HiT entertainment

Illustrations © Orchard Books 2013

A CIP catalogue record for this book is available
from the British Library.

ISBN 978 1 40832 502 5

1 3 5 7 9 10 8 6 4 2

Printed in Great Britain

The paper and board used in this paperback are natural recyclable
products made from wood grown in sustainable forests. The
manufacturing processes conform to the environmental regulations
of the country of origin.

Orchard Books is a division of Hachette Children's Books,
an Hachette UK company

www.hachette.co.uk

Nina
the Birthday Cake
Fairy

by Daisy Meadows

ORCHARD

www.rainbowmagic.co.uk

The Fairyland Palace

Candy Land

Goblins' ice cream van

Market sta

Charlie's ice cream va

Kirsty's Hous

Wetherbury Village

Jack Frost's Spell

I have a plan to cause some strife
And use those fairies to change my life.
I'm going to take their charms away
And make my dreams come true today!

I'll build a castle made of sweets,
And spoil the fairies' silly treats.
I just don't care how much they whine,
Their cakes and lollies will be mine!

Contents

Cake Calamity

"What an amazing birthday this has been!" said Kirsty Tate, doing a twirl in the middle of the pavement.

"It's been the best birthday ever," agreed her best friend Rachel Walker. "I've enjoyed it just as much as you, even though it's not MY birthday!"

Rachel was visiting the Tate family for the spring half term, and they were all walking home with Kirsty's parents from Wetherbury Park, where they had been celebrating Kirsty's birthday at the village funfair.

"So what's been the best thing about your birthday?" asked Mr Tate.

Kirsty threw her hands into the air.

"I can't decide!" she said with a laugh. "Everything has been perfect.

Rachel's here for a visit, Aunt Harri gave us a guided tour of *Candy Land*, and we've had a brilliant time at the funfair."

"Well, your birthday is about to get even better," said Mrs Tate.

Kirsty stopped and looked at her parents and her best friend. Their eyes were sparkling with happiness.

"We've got another birthday surprise for you," Mr Tate added.

Kirsty looked at their smiling faces in excitement.

"You have to tell me what the surprise is!" she pleaded.

Rachel shook her head. "That would spoil it," she said. "Come on, let's hurry back home."

The girls held hands and rushed ahead.

"It's really hard to keep secrets from you," Rachel said in a breathless voice. "We usually share all our secrets, don't we?"

The girls shared one of the biggest secrets imaginable. They were friends of Fairyland, and their latest magical adventures were some of the most thrilling they had ever had.

"My birthday would be absolutely perfect if we could just help the last Sweet Fairy get her magical charm back from Jack Frost," said Kirsty.

Two days ago, Jack Frost and his mischievous goblins had stolen the magical charms that belonged to the seven Sweet Fairies. Honey the Sweet Fairy had come to ask the girls for their help.

"We've already found six of the Sweet Fairies' charms," said Rachel. "There's just one more to find."

The Sweet Fairies needed their magical charms to look after all kinds of delicious sweet treats in both Fairyland and in the human world. But Jack Frost wanted all the sweets for his special project – a giant Candy Castle! He gave the

Sweet Fairies' charms to his goblins for
safekeeping and ordered them to bring
back all the sweets from the human
world.

"The worst part of it is that today is
Treat Day in Fairyland," said Kirsty.
"If Queen Titania and King Oberon
haven't got sweets to put in the treat
baskets for the fairies, Treat Day will
have to be cancelled."

At that moment they reached Kirsty's
front door. Rachel gave her best friend's
hand a squeeze.

"Forget about Jack Frost for now," she
said. "We can think about how to find
the last charm later. Right now, your
last birthday treat is waiting!"

Kirsty's parents caught them up and
opened the door. As Kirsty stepped

inside, there was a loud shout.

"SURPRISE!"

Aunt Harri and all Kirsty's school friends jumped out, waving balloons and banners! Kirsty's mouth fell open and her eyes grew wide.

"A party?" she said in an amazed whisper. "I can't believe it. I had no idea!"

Everyone laughed and cheered, and then her friends pulled her into the sitting room. It was beautifully decorated with pink, yellow and turquoise balloons, rainbow-coloured bunting and a big "Happy Birthday Kirsty" banner.

"This is fantastic," said Kirsty. "Thank you all so much!"

"Happy birthday!" said Rachel, giving Kirsty a big hug.

"Come into the kitchen and see your cake," said Aunt Harri, her eyes shining.

She led the girls into the kitchen, and they saw a large box sitting on the worktop. It was a cake box from the best bakery in the village, *Cupcake Corner*. Kirsty clapped her hands together with pleasure.

"I love *Cupcake Corner*!" she exclaimed.

Aunt Harri grinned at her.

"Then you're in for a treat," she said. "Ta-dah!"

She flung open the box and then gasped with dismay. Instead of a beautiful cake, there were only a few crumbs inside!

A Surprise in the Shed

"I can't understand where the cake could have gone," said Aunt Harri, frowning. "Maybe someone has taken it to put candles on. I'll go and check."

She hurried out of the kitchen. Just then there was a shout from Kirsty's friend Myla in the sitting room.

"Musical chairs!" she called. "Come on, everyone!"

Soon Kirsty and Rachel were alone in the kitchen. They exchanged a worried look.

"This must be the work of Jack Frost and his goblins," said Rachel.

As the music started up in the next room, Kirsty leaned over the cake box and examined it.

"I wonder if they've left any clues," she said.

Just then, the musical chairs music stopped. In the silence, the girls heard a soft sob.

"That sounded like a fairy," said Rachel in an excited voice.

"That bit of icing is glowing," said Kirsty, pointing to the corner of the box.

Then, to their delight, a tiny fairy peeped out from behind the blob of icing.

"It's Nina the Birthday Cake Fairy," exclaimed Rachel. "Hello, Nina!"

But Nina could hardly speak. Sparkly fairy tears were running down her face.

"Oh girls," she said, sniffing. "I feel so helpless! I've just seen Jack Frost steal your birthday cake, Kirsty, and I couldn't stop him. He's got my magic birthday candle charm! I'm so sorry."

The girls couldn't bear to see Nina so
upset. They wished that they were fairy-
sized so that they could put their arms
around her.

"Please don't cry," said Kirsty. "We'll
help you to get your charm back."

"Hey, look!" said Rachel in an excited
voice. "There are some crumbs outside
the box too."

"It looks like a trail,"
said Kirsty. "Come on,
we might be able to catch
up with Jack Frost!"

At once, Nina brushed
her tears away. She
zoomed into the air,
looking very determined.
She hid in the pocket of Kirsty's
skirt and the girls looked at each other.

In the sitting room, the music had started up again.

"No one will miss us yet," said Rachel. "They're all enjoying the party. Hopefully we can be back before they realise we've gone!"

The trail of crumbs led out of the back door and across the garden. Rachel and Kirsty ran lightly across the grass, following the delicious-looking crumbs until they reached the garden shed.

"Look, the door's half open,"
whispered Kirsty. "Mum and Dad
always close it. There must be someone
inside!"

They poked their heads around the
door. Inside, someone was standing
with his back to them. He was wearing
an ice-blue cape and his hair was very
spiky.

"Jack Frost," said Kirsty under her
breath.

"And look what's beside him," Rachel
whispered.

On an upturned crate was a glittering,
pink birthday cake. On the top, in
rose-pink icing, were the words 'Happy
Birthday Kirsty'.

Jack Frost was rubbing his hands
together and cackling with laughter.

"It can be my birthday every day now that I've got Nina's magic charm," he gloated. "I'm going to have the biggest birthday party EVER at my Candy Castle, with lots of presents and birthday songs, and I'll have ALL the sweets in Fairyland and in the human world. Best of all, I'll have mountains of birthday cake! It serves those interfering fairies right. Ha!"

He raised his wand and zapped the
birthday cake with a blast of icy magic.
The rose-pink icing seemed to dribble
and run, and was replaced with ice-blue
writing that said 'Happy Birthday Jack
Frost'.

Rachel couldn't bear to watch any
more. She felt angry and upset for her
best friend. She pushed open the shed
door and marched inside. Her eyes were
blazing.

"Stop that cackling right now," she said. "Give Kirsty's birthday cake back. You're spoiling her birthday!"

"Give back Nina's magic charm too," added Kirsty, hurrying into the shed after Rachel. "You have to stop being so mean, or else all birthday cakes everywhere will be ruined."

"I don't care!" shouted Jack Frost. He cackled again and hurled a bolt of magic at them. The girls dived out of the way, and then there was a loud BANG and a puff of blue smoke.

When the smoke cleared, Jack Frost had disappeared. And so had the birthday cake!

Instantly, Nina waved her wand and the girls were caught up in a candy-coloured swirl of fairy dust. They felt themselves shrinking to fairy-size, and wriggled their shoulders happily as fairy wings appeared on their backs. When the fairy dust cleared, they found themselves hovering high above Fairyland.

"It's wonderful to be back here!" said Rachel, doing a somersault in the air.

"I love being a fairy," added Kirsty with a laugh, shaking a few colourful specks of fairy dust from her hair.

"There's Jack Frost's Candy Castle," said Nina, pointing down to the cupcake turrets and the doors made of cookies. "Girls, this could be dangerous. Are you sure you want to come with me?"

"Of course!" said Rachel in a brave voice. "We're not letting Jack Frost spoil Treat Day. Or Kirsty's birthday!"

Jack Frost's Birthday

The girls and Nina flew towards the castle as fast as they could. They landed on the branch of a tree made of chocolate and looked up. The castle loomed high above them, rising out of the milkshake moat that surrounded the grounds.

"That's funny," said Rachel. "Even though the castle is brand new, it looks as if it's crumbling."

"Perhaps the goblin builders are there to repair it," said Kirsty.

She pointed to dozens of goblins who were standing around the castle walls. They were all dressed in green overalls with green hard hats, and they were standing very close to the walls.

"They're not building it," said Kirsty. "They're EATING it!"

She was right. The naughty goblins were sneaking bites of the Candy Castle!

"There were goblins eating the castle yesterday too," Rachel said. "Remember, Kirsty? We saw them when we came here with Clara the Chocolate Fairy."

"Yes," said Kirsty. "Goodness, it looks terrible! It's covered in bite-shaped holes."

Nina gave a sudden sharp gasp.

"Look down, girls!" she whispered.

Below them, a long-nosed goblin was nibbling on the trunk of the chocolate tree. He had pieces of dark-chocolate bark in each hand, and chocolate-milk sap was running down his chin.

"Jack Frost's Candy Castle will disappear in days if the greedy goblins carry on like this," said Rachel.

Just then, they heard a bell ringing. The gates of the Candy Castle opened, and out came a goblin dressed as a town crier. He was wearing a black three-cornered hat topped by a white feather, a long red-and-gold cape, black knickerbockers and a pair of white tights. He was carrying a large bell. The other goblins all stopped eating the castle and stared at him. Then they started giggling and pointing.

The town crier goblin stuck his tongue out at them and rang his bell again.

"Hear ye, hear ye!" he bellowed. "Today is Jack Frost's birthday. Every goblin is ordered to come to the marquee in the garden to sing 'Happy Birthday'. Presents are required. Any goblin who doesn't come will be in BIG TROUBLE. There will be birthday cake!"

As soon as they heard the word "cake", the other goblins stopped giggling. They all raced towards the marquee, elbowing each other out of the way.

35

The girls could see the top of the marquee from their hiding place in the tree.

"It looks as though it's made of icing," said Kirsty.

Nina nodded sadly. "It's fondant icing," she said. "Jack Frost has taken all the loveliest sweet treats. Come on, let's follow the goblins to the marquee. If that's where Jack Frost is, then that's where my charm and Kirsty's cake are too!"

The three friends fluttered into the air and zoomed after the goblins. They flew high above the moat so they wouldn't be seen. The goblins looked like tiny green specks below. As they disappeared into the marquee, the girls hovered side by side and looked at each other.

"We have to go inside," said Rachel.

The others nodded, looking nervous.
They waited until the last goblin had
entered the marquee.
Then they held
hands and
swooped down
through the
entrance.

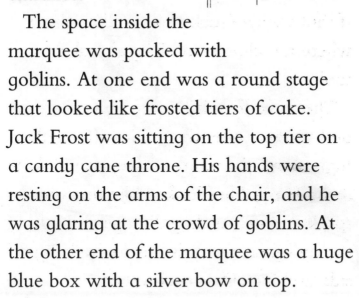

The space inside the
marquee was packed with
goblins. At one end was a round stage
that looked like frosted tiers of cake.
Jack Frost was sitting on the top tier on
a candy cane throne. His hands were
resting on the arms of the chair, and he
was glaring at the crowd of goblins. At
the other end of the marquee was a huge
blue box with a silver bow on top.

"Look," said Nina in a whisper.

"Kirsty's birthday cake is on the table in front of Jack Frost!"

"And your magical birthday candle charm is on that chain around his wrist," added Kirsty.

"But just look at all the goblins in here," said Rachel. How are we going to get it back?"

Just then, the town crier goblin climbed onto the lowest tier of the cake stage and rang his bell. Nina, Kirsty and Rachel hid behind a large bunch of balloons made of bubble-gum bubbles. They were very close to the long-nosed goblin who had been eating the chocolate tree.

"Listen!" the town crier squawked. "All goblins will now sing 'Happy Birthday', led by everyone's favourite musicians."

He pointed at the big blue box at the far end of the marquee. With an explosion of silver glitter, Frosty's Gobolicious Band burst out of the box and started to sing!

Fairies Under Attack!

As all the goblins joined in the song, the girls covered their ears. Every goblin seemed to be singing a different song to a different tune! Rachel couldn't help but giggle when she heard the words that the long-nosed goblin was singing:

"Happy birthday to you,
Mashed potatoes and stew!
You look like an elephant,
And you smell like one too!"

Luckily, Jack Frost didn't hear him.
The Ice Lord leaned forward and blew
out the candles on the cake. Then there
was a stampede! All the goblins wanted a
piece of birthday cake. They scampered
up the steps of the stage, and then Jack
Frost sprang to his feet with a yell.

"STOP!" he bellowed.

The goblins froze. Some of them had
started to drool. Their master's eyes were
blazing with temper.

"No one is having any birthday cake until I get some PRESENTS!" Jack Frost shouted.

The goblins looked down and shuffled their feet.

"The thing is…"

"It was such short notice…"

"We haven't had much time…"

"NOT GOOD ENOUGH!" roared Jack Frost.

In desperation, the town crier goblin leaned forward and puckered up his lips.

"Would you like a birthday kiss, my lord?"

"Ugh!" bawled Jack Frost.

He shoved the goblin backwards and he fell on top of three other goblins. Nina, Rachel and Kirsty put their hands over their mouths to stifle their giggles.

"You can give me my presents later," announced Jack Frost. "Band, play 'For He's a Jolly Good Fellow' – NOW!"

The band struck up and the goblins made a half-hearted attempt to sing along. But they were impatient for a bit of birthday cake, and some of them couldn't wait any longer. The girls saw them start to lick the candy-cane throne.

"Stop that, you greedy guts!" Jack Frost demanded. "Fine, come and get your share of the cake."

"Oh no!" exclaimed Nina.

Jack Frost cut the thinnest slivers of cake that he could and handed them out to the goblins. Then he picked up a big chunk of cake and opened his mouth wide. The charm glinted around his wrist. Seeing it again was too much for Nina.

"I want my charm back!" she cried.

She darted out from behind the
balloons and zoomed towards Jack Frost.
Rachel and Kirsty were close behind her.
Everyone was so busy eating cake that
they didn't see the three fairies coming.
Nina zipped down beside Jack Frost's
hand and started to undo the chain
that held the charm. Rachel and Kirsty

held their breath
in excitement,
fluttering above
in case Nina
needed them.
Could she get
the charm back
without anyone
noticing?

Just then, Jack Frost tilted his head back to tip more cake into his mouth and saw Rachel and Kirsty hovering above his head.

"Fairies!" he snarled, raising his wand. "We're infested with fairies!"

He sent a bolt of icy magic crackling towards them, and Rachel and Kirsty were hurled sideways.

"Stop that!" cried Nina. "Leave them alone!"

47

She grabbed on to his wand, trying to drag it out of his hands. Jack Frost gave a mean laugh and flicked the wand, sending Nina tumbling away across the marquee.

"You'll never get your charm back!" he shouted.

Rachel and Kirsty caught Nina, who shook her head dizzily.

"Look out!" cried Kirsty.

They just managed to dodge another thunderbolt of magic, which hit the bubble-gum balloons behind them. There was a huge bang and all the balloons burst, covering the goblins in a sticky mess.

"My knickerbockers!" squealed the town crier.

The other goblins tried to pull his

clothes off, but they just got stuck
together. Every time they touched
anything, they stuck to it! Amid the
squawks and wails of the goblins, Jack
Frost grabbed the rest of the cake and
dashed out of the marquee.

"Follow him!" cried Rachel. "We
mustn't let him out of our sight!"

The Ice Lord Takes a Dip

The fairies flew after Jack Frost as he ran cackling into the Candy Castle. He stumbled over broken cobbles made of gobstoppers, and then raced up a winding nougat staircase to the battlements at the top of the tallest tower. The fairies were close behind him, but as soon as they flew out of the stairwell, Jack Frost flung a barrage of hailstones at them, stinging their faces and hands.

The fairies took cover behind the
parapet and tried to catch
their breath.

"You'll never stop me
now," Jack Frost gloated,
through a mouthful of
birthday cake. "Your
charm is mine for ever!"

He patted the charm that was still
dangling around his wrist and shoved
another piece of cake into his mouth.

"What are we going to do?" asked
Nina. "As long as he has his wand, we
can't get close to him!"

"Perhaps we don't need to," said Kirsty
thoughtfully. "Remember how angry he
got when the goblins licked his candy-
cane throne? Perhaps if we eat some of
his castle, he might forget to be so careful

about the charm."

They all flew down the side of
the tower and hovered below the
battlements, close to a small window.
The frame of the window was made of
toffee and raisin fudge. Kirsty winked at
Rachel and Nina.

"Mmm!" she said in a loud voice.
"These window frames are delicious!"

"Scrumptious!" added Rachel at the
top of her voice. "Maybe we should just
forget about the charm and eat up the
Candy Castle instead."

"STOP THAT!" Jack
Frost roared, leaning
over the battlements.

The fairies looked
up and rubbed their
tummies.

"I've never tasted such wonderful fudge," said Nina, licking her lips.

"Leave that window frame alone!" Jack Frost shrieked. "It's MINE!"

"We'll leave right now if you'll give back Nina's charm," said Kirsty.

"NO DEAL!" Jack Frost snarled.

He sent magic bolts raining down on them, but the fairies just pressed themselves against the wall and laughed.

"You can't stop us eating," called Rachel, pretending to pick off a piece of windowsill. "You can't reach us from up there."

"Oh, CAN'T I?" the Ice Lord replied.

He leaned so far over the battlements that he nearly fell off. As he pointed his wand downwards, trying to aim at the fairies, the charm slipped off his wrist and he dropped his wand!

"NOOO!" Jack Frost wailed as the chain and magical charm plummeted downwards.

"Catch the charm!" cried Nina.

Rachel zoomed over, but she was half a second too late. The  charm was still falling. She would have flown after it, but suddenly there was a shriek from above. Jack Frost had leaned out even further, and the battlement wall had started to crumble.

"The wall has been weakened by the goblins' nibbles," said Kirsty with a gasp. "It's full of holes!"

Before Nina could raise her wand to help, the wall collapsed and Jack Frost hurtled down with it, the birthday cake following close behind.

"HELP!" he wailed.

He disappeared into the moat with a gigantic SPLASH! Frothy milkshake flew into the air and covered the banks of the moat. The fairies zoomed down and saw Jack Frost bob to the surface. He spat out a mouthful of milkshake and thrashed about wildly.

"Help!" he shouted again. "Come here, you useless goblins! Get me out of here!"

But all his goblins were still stuck together with bubble-gum in the marquee. Kirsty pointed to something brown lying on the bank.

"There's a branch of the chocolate tree that's been nibbled off," she exclaimed. "We could use it to pull him out!"

Together the three fairies flew to the middle of the moat and held the branch out to Jack Frost.

"Grab the end of this and we'll pull you to the shore," Rachel said.

He clutched at the branch and the fairies hauled him to the bank of the moat. As he lay there, gasping and soggy, the three friends looked at each other.

"Jack Frost is safe," said Kirsty. "But where is Nina's magic charm?"

"It must have sunk in the moat," said Nina, holding back her tears. "Oh girls, it's gone for ever!"

Treat Day in Fairyland

The girls held Nina's hands, feeling very sad. Then, out of the corner of her eye, Rachel saw something glinting on the frothy surface of the moat.

"Maybe not!" she said, darting out above the moat again.

The milkshake bubbles were making the little birthday candle charm dance on the surface. It looked almost as if the moat were playing with it! Rachel reached the shining charm and scooped it up. Then she flew back to the bank and handed it to Nina. The charm immediately shrank to fairy-size, and Nina's eyes welled up with happy tears as she slipped it onto her wrist.

"I can't believe it!" she said. "All seven of the Sweet Fairies' charms are back where they belong!"

"Yes, and look what's happening to the Candy Castle," said Kirsty.

As they watched, Jack Frost's new castle seemed to melt away. Jack leapt to his feet and jumped up and down in fury. On the other side of the moat he could see the sticky goblins crawling out of the marquee, picking up the last traces of sweets.

"Stop that!" he hollered. "Those sweets are mine, do you hear me? MINE!"

"Hasn't all this taught you a lesson?" Rachel asked him. "You shouldn't be so greedy!"

He just shook his fist at her.

"I think it's time for us to leave," said Nina with a laugh.

She waved her wand, and in a twinkling of fairy dust the girls were standing in the Fairyland Sweet Factory. It was an orchard where sweets grew on trees, and the last time they had been here it had been a very sad place. Because Jack Frost had stolen the Sweet Fairies' charms, the sweets had all been ruined.

"What a difference!" said Kirsty, looking around in relief.

The boughs of the trees were heavy with sweets. It was a wonderful crop. Fat bunches of lemon sherbets, orange creams and strawberry fondants hung from the branches. The six other Sweet

Fairies were there already, busily filling the Treat Day baskets. When they saw the girls and Nina, they sped over and shared a big fairy hug, their wings fluttering together.

"You did it!" cheered Madeleine the Cookie Fairy. "When the orchard came back to life we knew you must have been helping Nina. Thank you!"

"Yes," said a beautiful voice behind them. "We thank you from the bottom of our hearts."

The fairies turned and saw Queen Titania and King Oberon smiling at them. Honey the Sweet Fairy was at their side, and their arms were filled with baskets of gooey macaroons, oaty cookies, handmade chocolates and prettily decorated muffins.

"We're here to complete the Treat Day baskets," Queen Titania went on. "We're so grateful for your help, Kirsty and Rachel. Treat Day would not be happening without you. Once again you have shown us that you are Fairyland's best friends."

"There's a big slice of birthday cake going into each fairy's basket in honour of your birthday, Kirsty," added Honey.

"Thank you for everything," said Nina, giving them a final hug. "But now it's time for you to go back to the human world. There's a party waiting for you!"

67

She winked and
raised her wand.
A flurry of
rainbow-
coloured fairy
dust swirled
around the
girls and lifted
them into the
air. When the
sparkles faded away,
they were back in Kirsty's kitchen. The
music was still playing for musical chairs
in the next room, and they heard the
doorbell ringing.

"No time has passed at all," said
Rachel in wonder, looking up at the
clock. "That's one of the most wonderful
things about Fairyland."

"Yes," said Kirsty, smiling at her best friend, "and it means that my birthday lasts even longer!"

Aunt Harri came hurrying into the kitchen with another box from *Cupcake Corner*.

"This has just been delivered," she said in an excited voice. "Look, girls! They must have heard that something had happened to the first one. This one's even prettier!"

She lifted the box lid and Rachel and Kirsty peered inside. They saw another rose-pink birthday cake that said "Happy Birthday Kirsty" on it, just like the one that Jack Frost had stolen. But this one had seven little fairies on it made of fondant icing…seven little fairies who looked very familiar. Kirsty and Rachel shared a secret smile. The fairies on the cake looked just like the Sweet Fairies!

Aunt Harri put the cake on a plate and lit the candles. Then she dimmed the lights, and all Kirsty's friends and family came into the kitchen to sing "Happy Birthday". Kirsty closed her eyes and made a special birthday wish. Then she blew out the candles.

As everyone cheered and the lights went on, Rachel squeezed Kirsty's hand. "What did you wish for?" she asked.

"I can't tell you that, or it won't happen," said Kirsty with a laugh. "And this is a wish I really want to come true!"

But Rachel could guess what her best friend had wished for. They both wanted more magical fun with their fairy friends...and they hoped that another adventure was just around the corner!

"I can't believe we're actually at holiday
camp together!" Rachel Walker said
happily.

"Me, neither," said her best friend,
Kirsty Tate. "We can do some of our
favourite things all in one place. And we
get to do them together!"

Rachel and Kirsty had met on holiday
on the beautiful Rainspell Island. Since
they lived in different towns, they didn't
get to see each other every day. So when
the girls' parents had suggested they go
to Camp Oakwood, both Rachel and
Kirsty were very excited.

Now, on their second day of camp, the two girls sat at a table in the Craft Cabin. They were making pictures with wool.

"First, sketch your picture on the paper," explained Bollie, their camp leader. Bollie's real name was Margaret Bolleran, but everyone called her Bollie.

Rachel sketched a fairy on her paper. She looked over at Kirsty and saw that she had sketched a fairy, too. The girls smiled at each other.

"Now spread the glue over the places you would normally colour in," Bollie said. "Then you can curl up pieces of wool and place them on the glue, like this."

She held up a picture of a tree with green wool for leaves and brown wool on the trunk...but then the wool slid off and plopped on one of Bollie's boots.

"That's funny," she said, feeling the paper. "This glue isn't sticky at all."

"My glue isn't sticking, either," complained a red-haired girl.

Bollie frowned. "Maybe it's too hot," she said. "I know! Let's have some fun with the paint spinner, instead."

Bollie walked to a big machine on a table at the side of the room. Rachel, Kirsty and the other girls gathered around to watch.

"It's easy," Bollie said, her green eyes shining. "You put paper on the bottom. Then you turn on the spinner and squeeze in drops of paint."

She held a plastic bottle of orange paint over the spinner and squeezed it. But with a POP the lid slipped off!

Read Nicki the Holiday Camp Fairy to find out what adventures are in store for Kirsty and Rachel!

Meet the
Sweet Fairies

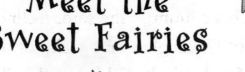

If Kirsty and Rachel don't find
the Sweet Fairies' magical charms,
Jack Frost will ruin all sweet treats for ever!

www.rainbowmagicbooks.co.uk

Meet the fairies, play games
and get sneak peeks at
the latest books!

www.rainbowmagicbooks.co.uk

There's fairy fun for everyone on
our wonderful website.
You'll find great activities, competitions, stories and
fairy profiles, and also a special newsletter.

Get 30% off all Rainbow Magic books at

www.rainbowmagicbooks.co.uk

Enter the code RAINBOW at the checkout.
Offer ends 31 December 2013.

Offer valid in United Kingdom and Republic of Ireland only.

Competition!

The Sweet Fairies have created a special competition just for you!
In the back of each book in the Sweet Fairies series there will
be a question for you to answer. First you need to collect the
answer from the back of each book in the series.
Once you have all the answers, take the first letter from each one
and arrange them to spell a secret word!
When you have the answer, go online and enter!

We will put all the correct entries into a draw and select a winner
to receive a special Rainbow Magic Goodie Bag featuring lots of
treats for you and your fairy friends. You'll also star in a new
Rainbow Magic story!

What sort of shop does Tracy Twist run in the Sweet Fairies series?

_ _ _ _ _ _

Enter online now at www.rainbowmagicbooks.co.uk

Nicki the
Holiday Camp
Fairy

Rachel and Kirsty have been looking forward to camp, but everything is going wrong. Can they help Nicki fix things, before the whole summer is ruined?

www.rainbowmagicbooks.co.uk